Going Home

Going Home

K. M. Peyton

Philomel Books
New York

First published in the United States in 1982 by Philomel Books,
a division of The Putnam Publishing Group, 51 Madison
Avenue, New York, New York 10010. Published in Great
Britain by Oxford University Press, 1982.
Copyright © 1982 by K. M. Peyton.

Library of Congress Cataloging in Publication Data
Peyton, K. M.
Going home.
Summary: Shortly after arriving in France on a
holiday, two homesick English children run away from
their temporary guardians and set off for their home and
mother who is recovering from a breakdown.
[1. Brothers and sisters — Fiction.   2. Runaways —
Fiction]   I. Title.
PZ7.P4483Go   1982   [Fic]   81-22703
ISBN 0-399-20889-5   AACR2

Going Home

One

They were sent to stay with Auntie Jackie and Uncle Kevin because their mother had had to go into the hospital. They were taken there in the social worker's car, sitting close together on the back seat, silent and unwilling.

"It'll be a nice trip for you, going on holiday with them," Fred said cheerily. "You'll like that."

"It's France," Milly said, disagreeing.

"Going abroad at your age—it's great."

"I don't want to go abroad," Milly said.

"I want to go home," Micky said.

He always said that when they were away. They went away often, Milly and Micky, as they were what the welfare council called a problem family. Their father had left home a long time ago and

9

every so often their mother went off to look for him, leaving Milly and Micky behind. Only the council considered this a problem, as Milly did not mind staying at home looking after Micky. "You're too young," they said, and they would send the social worker, Fred, to collect them.

Sometimes they were sent to live with various relatives, or sometimes even to a foster home until their mother came to pick them up. They didn't like it. If Micky was parted from Milly he screamed until she turned up again. Even at school he was quite often sent to sit with her, although she was two grades higher. He just sat there, sucking his thumb, no trouble, but when he screamed his screams could be heard all over the school. He was always sent to Milly when he screamed.

"Boy like you," Fred said now to Micky, "will do fine on this holiday—you're going in a boat, they say. A boat on a canal."

The only canal Micky knew was the Regents Park-through-Islington near where they lived, and it wasn't what he thought of as a holiday place. It was lined with warehouses and demolition dumps. Holidays, he thought, ought to be like on the television: bright blue swimming pools in hot sunshine and ladies in bikinis running along a beach. But perhaps that was what it was like abroad. Perhaps all those places on the television were abroad.

"Will there be television?" he asked Milly.

"I shouldn't think so," she said. "And if there is it will talk funny."

10

"How?"

"French."

French was something he had heard of at school. It was a subject you could take if you were a good student. Micky wasn't. Milly was, but hadn't got to French yet. She was only nine.

"I don't mind going if there's television," he said. It didn't matter if it talked funny. He liked the pictures. He didn't listen most of the time anyway.

There was a television at Auntie Jackie and Uncle Kevin's. It was huge and everyone had bright purple faces. Micky sat in front of it entranced. He heard Auntie Jackie say,

"Well, he's a rascal, turning on the TV without so much as a how do you do!"

Milly said, "He's good when he's watching TV." Her voice was worried.

"Isn't he good when he's not watching TV then?" Uncle Kevin asked brightly.

Milly did not answer. She was feeling a bit panicky, being in this new house and Micky all her own responsibility now, with Fred about to depart. Fred looked worried too. The house was very stylish and tidy, and her aunt and uncle were stylish to match, not like the people Milly was used to. All the cushions were plumped up and the ashtrays empty. There was wall-to-wall carpeting and it was thick and soft and patterned with red roses. It was lovely to sit on.

11

"Sit up on the settee now," Auntie Jackie said, "and I'll get some tea."

"We're going away tomorrow," Uncle Kevin said. "You'll like that, won't you? Never had a proper holiday before, have you?"

It was difficult to say they didn't want one. Milly wanted to stay with the carpet and Micky with the television. They did not reply, unable to say the right thing.

Fred said, "They'll be all right when they've settled. Leave the little boy to Milly if he—if he misbehaves. And you've got my telephone number, just in case."

"That sounds ominous," Auntie Jackie said with a light laugh. "They are only little—not as if it's teenagers. I'm sure we can handle them."

Fred did not answer.

"Goodbye, kids. Have a good time."

He gave Milly a sort of shake around the shoulders and bent down and said softly, "I'm always there if you want me, remember. Not far away."

"We're going abroad," Milly said.

"When you come back, I mean. After your holiday."

"I don't want a holiday."

"No. Well."

He straightened up, his face blank, and went out to his car.

Auntie Jackie saw him out and came back,

saying, "What would you like for your tea now? Some nice scrambled eggs?"

"French fries," Micky said.

"I don't make French fries. The smell gets in the curtains," Auntie Jackie said.

She went out to make scrambled eggs, which Milly knew neither of them would eat. Uncle Kevin said, "Come on, Milly, I'll show you your bedroom."

They went upstairs, up thick, sinky carpet and Uncle Kevin showed her a bedroom for herself and a bedroom for Micky. They were pink and pretty, with frilled pillowcases and great fluffy eiderdown things for blankets.

"We always sleep together."

"Well, it's luxury here then! A room each."

Milly knew they would still sleep together, whatever happened, and if she wasn't jolly careful Micky would wet the bed. She lifted up the eiderdown thing and saw the undersheet, pink with little roses all over it. She sighed.

"Don't you like it?"

"Yes, it's lovely."

She was frightened of what they would say. Even nice untidy people they stayed with got cross. If Auntie Jackie didn't like the smell of French fries she wouldn't like the smell of Micky either, in the morning.

Uncle Kevin showed her the bathroom. It had a pink tub and was huge, and carpet all over, just like the living room. She took her opportunity and stayed in, locking the door, and Uncle Kevin left her and went downstairs. A few minutes alone, to think, were very necessary.

"Milly! Milly! Whatever are you doing?" Her aunt's voice came up the stairs.

Milly went down and sat on the floor again by Micky.

"Do you always sit on the floor?" Auntie Jackie asked her.

"No." Floor at home was scratchy and not very clean.

"Come and sit up then. You must be hungry."

There was absolutely nothing on the table that either of them considered eatable, only the scrambled eggs and dull homemade cake. No French fries, no ketchup, no beans, no sliced bread, no potato chips. They sat mutely, swinging their legs. Their aunt and uncle were cross and tried every ploy from coaxing to threats, but Milly and Micky had no doubts about winning. One stuck it out, saying nothing. One always won.

"You won't sleep, you'll be hungry in the night! No wonder you're such little sticks, both of you! I don't know how Maggie treats you, to have you so finicky!"

Maggie was their mother.

"She gives us proper food," Micky said.

"Junk food, I daresay!" Auntie Jackie's voice was so contemptuous of their mother that Milly's feelings hardened against her.

14

"You can't watch the television if you don't eat," Uncle Kevin said to Micky.

"I want to watch television."

"Not if you don't eat."

Milly began to feel her familiar worries rising. It was all going to happen, she knew it, and there was only going to be her to cope. She looked at Micky, at his white, closed face, the dark, staring, adamant eyes. He was always the same, whomever he had to face, holding steadfastly to his will. He never wavered.

Auntie Jackie cleared away in silent rage. Milly helped her. She scraped the scrambled eggs into the garbage for her and put the cake back in its tin, as helpful as possible. She was listening to Uncle Kevin, turning on the television and telling Micky to go and sit in the other room. Poor Uncle Kevin, she thought sadly.

She heard the scuffle of force being used, the door shutting, opening again, the cheerful voices of television carrying on regardless. The door slammed fiercely. Micky began to scream.

Auntie Jackie stood petrified at the sink.

"Good heavens!"

Milly wiped the plate stolidly.

There came the sounds of Uncle Kevin's agitation, clumps and shouts.

"Whatever's wrong?" Auntie Jackie asked.

"He always does that," Milly said.

"Can't you stop him?"

"Not really, no. Only give him what he wants."

15

She did not like to say that he did not do it when his mother was there, as it seemed rude. Only when they were at other people's, and at school sometimes.

Auntie Jackie was beginning to look distraught, a look that was familiar to Milly.

"He'll stop if you let him watch the television," Milly said. It seemed to her quite a simple solution.

"He always gets what he wants then?" snapped Auntie Jackie.

But he didn't want anything at home. Milly could not answer.

They let him watch the television.

"After all," Auntie Jackie said to her husband over their heads, "it's not our job to train him. It's only a temporary arrangement."

"I only hope they're not going to ruin our holiday," Uncle Kevin said.

Milly hoped so too. When they went to bed she arranged with Micky for him to come into her bed when they were left alone. He did so, and she stayed awake most of the night to make sure he didn't wet the bed. It was very wearing, life without their mother.

The next day they set off for France. They drove to Weymouth, where they left the car, met some friends called Auntie Marilyn and Uncle Kit, and went on board the ferry for St. Malo. Micky was fascinated by everything he saw, having scarcely ever left the boroughs of Hackney and Islington in all his life. He had seen boats on the Thames and

on the Regents Park canal, but never boats like this one, nor yachts, let alone the sea. They went on board and watched the cars driving up the ramp and into the great open jaw of their ship. Some of them towed trailers that had the letters GB painted on the back.

"What's GB for?" Micky asked.

"It means Great Britain," Milly said.

She wished they had a trailer. It was like taking a little piece of home away with you, like a tortoise, so wherever you were you had your own patch of Great Britain, comfy chairs and baked beans in the cupboard, plastic flowers and a portable television set. She was frightened of going abroad. The sea stretched into infinity, bleak and blue and smooth.

She looked away from it back at the cars loading, and saw a small red trailer coming on board, very trim, with looped net curtains and parakeets in a cage on the table. In the car were an elderly man and his wife, both fat and red-faced, like garden gnomes. She wouldn't have minded going abroad with them. They had such an aura of comfiness about them that in their company, living in their trailer, one would be as good as at home. Milly dreaded the sea that was about to separate her from her mother.

"I don't want to go," she said to Auntie Jackie. She was frightened of crying.

"You'll love it, dear! Don't worry. It will be a lovely holiday for you, just what you need."

18

Micky gazed and gazed at the cars feeding the great open jaws of their boat. It was not Micky that Milly was worried for any more, only herself.

"Mummy's not going to die, is she?"

Auntie Jackie laughed. "She's only tired, and mixed up—she's gone for a rest! She's not *ill* at all."

"Why didn't she come on this holiday then? It would have made her better."

"Oh dear, the questions you ask! Go and buy yourself a bag of potato chips."

She gave Milly some money and a little shove. Milly went and stood at the rail and looked at the sea. The boat closed its jaws and started to move. Milly watched England receding beyond the wide white curve of the ship's wake, the downs and cliffs and little houses. The sea between their boat and the shore stretched irrevocably wider, until the houses grew blurry and the white cliffs dimmed and all one could see was a furry blue haze.

Aunties Jackie and Marilyn and Uncles Kevin and Kit were in the bar, having drinks and laughing a lot. Micky was trying to find a way down into the hold where the cars were. Milly sat on a bench and wished she belonged to the little red trailer. If she *had* to come abroad, the trailer would have made it bearable. As it was, she could not see that it was going to be bearable at all. She kept feeling like crying, but knew she couldn't because she had Micky to look after.

It was a very long way. England disappeared

completely and France never seemed to come. The sea was smooth and serene, quite nice if you liked that sort of thing, but Milly did not like the extent of it, the farness of France from England. They had fish-and-chips for dinner, then Milly fell asleep, although she had not meant to. When she awoke, France was in sight, fuzzy and blue at first, and then gradually turning into a high rocky shore with a town like a great castle with walls around it. It looked like a fortress, to keep them at bay. "But I don't want to come," Milly thought, glowering at France. It was cool and nearly dark; crescents of golden sand shimmered like melon rinds below the walls. She was sent to find Micky in the hold. All the car drivers were going down, ready to drive off and Milly saw the garden gnomes going to their cozy trailer. She thought of the little room behind the lace curtains with the parakeets and wished it was for her and Micky. She looked out at the flickering lights on the pier and thought of this boat going back again to Weymouth, and she wanted to stay on board, in hiding, and go back to England. "But I can't," she thought. She had to look after Micky. She found him talking to a truck driver and dragged him away, back up the interminable stairs against the people coming down, back to where they were waiting to go ashore. She could not remember who was Auntie What or Uncle Who. They had blended together into a noisy, laughing band of people to whom, she could see plainly, she and Micky were a nuisance.

"Thought you were going to be all night!" they said, picking up their suitcases.

They all staggered off down the gangway into France, where it smelled funny and men were shouting at each other unintelligibly. Uncle Kevin went to fetch a taxi. The car had a sign on top that said "Taxi" in English but the driver could not talk English and Uncle Kevin could not talk French. They carried on for some time, each in his own language, and appeared to come to some understanding, for everyone climbed inside, the luggage was put in the trunk, and the driver roared away with them. It was a long drive. Micky fell asleep and Milly did too. Once she woke up and looked out of the window and saw a great sheet of water with the reflection of the moon in it. It seemed to be a river, for there were lights on the other side, far away. It looked very strange and lonely. She shut her eyes and a great pang of homesickness made her shiver. Uncle Kevin put his jacket over her, and she fell asleep again.

TWO

When Milly awoke in the morning, she found she was in a bunk on board a boat. But this time the boat was small—the six of them quite filled it—and it lay on a narrow river against a dock. She could lie in her bunk and look through a window and see women going past with shopping bags, a cat sunning itself, a man sweeping out the front of a café. It was warm and peaceful. But Milly's worries came back as soon as she came fully awake.

This was the boat that was going to take them into France down the canal, farther and farther away from England.

Auntie Jackie thought it was great. After they had breakfasted and shopped in the town, they cast off the mooring lines, Uncle Kevin started the engine, and Auntie Jackie called Milly to come and sit with her on the cabin top.

"We can see where we're going . . . sun our-selves. Let the men do all the work."

Uncle Kit coiled in the lines and Uncle Kevin stood at the wheel and steered the boat away from the dock. On either side of the canal, old gray houses climbed steeply up from the water's edge, and they passed under a road bridge that was hung high above them, carried on tall stone stilts. Under the bridge the houses gave way to woods and fields and the canal became very narrow so that the trees almost met overhead. It twisted and turned and Uncle Kevin had to throttle down the speed.

"Bloomin' 'eck! Call this a waterway? More like a ditch."

The trees came right down so that Milly could catch the branches. The dark green water snaked ahead, its edges fringed with rushes. Beyond the trees were fields of long grass full of buttercups and some cows grazing. It was very peaceful. In spite of its being France, Milly could not help thinking it was very nice. After a little while they came to a high stone dock and a small cottage by the water's edge, covered in untidy roses. There was a garden of soldierly vegetables, a lot of chickens scratching about, a dog in a kennel, and a bent old woman in a black dress. There were gates across the canal blocking their path. The sides of the canal seemed very high. They could hardly see over.

"Our first lock," Auntie Jackie said.

"What's a lock?" asked Micky.

"The land is going uphill," Uncle Kit said, "and to keep the water from running away they have to put gates across it every so often to keep it in. Like that."

The old lady was shouting to them.

"What the bloomin' 'eck's she saying?" Uncle Kevin muttered.

"You've got to tie the boat up, I think."

"That's it," said Uncle Kit, "and shut the other gates."

They gave Milly a rope to take ashore and wind around a post to keep the boat by the dock. The old lady pushed against a big wooden lever and a pair of gates closed behind their boat, so that it was completely enclosed, gates in front and gates behind. Then she went to the front gates and wound some levers and water started to gush in from the canal in front through some sluice gates, very fast and rushing, so that their boat tossed about. The level of the water in the canal beyond the gates was higher than the level below, but the water coming in raised the level in the lock. Their boat came up with it until it rode high and the dog could look in through the cabin windows. The water was now on a level with the water in front of them, and when Milly looked behind she saw that the water on the other side of the gates behind them was now much lower.

25

"It's like coming up in an elevator."

The old lady then opened the gates in front of them and the water stretched invitingly ahead.

"That's very clever, going upstairs in a boat," Milly said.

She marveled about it for quite some while, as the boat slipped on through woods and water-meadows.

But quite soon they came to another pair of gates and another cottage and another old lady in a black dress with a flowered apron. She shouted to them and made gestures with her skinny arms.

"I think we have to help her," Uncle Kit said, "wind down them levers or something."

After a while they got the idea, after ten more locks. They found that winding the ratchets to open the sluices was very hard work, although the little old ladies made it look very easy. Uncles Kevin and Kit sweated and muttered and got big blisters. Aunties Jackie and Marilyn held the ropes and got shouted at when they let go and the boat swung around in the rushing water and bumped the sides of the lock. The door of the food cupboard in the galley below swung open and all the food shot out onto the floor and a jar of marmalade broke.

"Call this a holiday? More like a labor camp!" Auntie Jackie moaned, seeing the mess. She had rope burns on her hands.

"If you'd made a proper turn around that post

it wouldn't have happened!" Uncle Kevin bawled down.

He opened up the throttle and their little boat surged on. Two more bends and they could see a pair of gates ahead blocking the way.

"Bloomin' 'eck," said Uncle Kevin.

"Better have a stop for lunch, eh?" Uncle Kit suggested. "Bit of a rest."

They shouted below, "We're stopping for lunch."

The engine stopped and the boat nosed gently into the rushes. The fields of long grass stretched as far as the eye could see, with old trees and high, straggling hedges making patches of shade. There was no sign of human habitation. Milly sat on the deck and watched bright blue dragonflies darting across the water. It was hot and peaceful and she was beginning to like it.

"Marilyn and I thought we'd eat out," Auntie Jackie said, coming up from below. "We are on holiday, after all."

"You'll eat out all right," Uncle Kevin said shortly. "Out on the bank. Or out on the deck. Take your choice."

"We meant a restaurant."

Uncle Kevin laughed unkindly. "Start walking!"

Milly could see that they were all tired and cross. They had a picnic instead, which cheered them up, but they were all agreed that if it was going to be like this it was more hard work than holiday.

"And it's so lonely," Auntie Jackie said plaintively. "Look at it!"

"Big place, France," Uncle Kit said. "Not so crowded as England."

"I thought we'd find a few discos—nice eating places and so on."

The more Auntie Jackie didn't like France, the more Milly did. She had never seen such tranquility, such miles of flower-strewn meadows and dozing cows. There were no towns, not even any villages, only the occasional sleepy farm up a leafy lane, and the lock keepers' cottages at distressingly frequent intervals. Once, the land rose up a steep wooded bank on one side and fell gently away on the other, and when Milly looked back she saw the gray roofs of what looked like an enchanted castle sticking out from the trees high above the canal. It had towers and turrets with tiny arched windows and was covered with green leaves like a picture out of a story book. In a few seconds, by a twist of the canal, it had vanished, and Milly wondered if she had seen it at all. The picture stayed in her mind long after it was gone in fact. "I would like to go there," she thought. "I would like to live there away from Auntie Jackie and them, peaceful and quiet."

The faster Uncle Kevin went, "to get to the bright lights," as he said, the harder the work of getting through the locks. One day they came to a "staircase" of eleven locks one after another. At the end of that Uncles Kevin and Kit and Aunties

Jackie and Marilyn had a great row about whose idea this holiday had been. There was nowhere for Milly and Micky to escape to and they had to endure the unpleasantness, sitting on their bunks in the tiny fo'c'sle where they slept.

Micky said, "I don't like it. I want to go home." He started to cry. "I want Mummy!"

"Oh, don't!" Milly said. She did too, with a really awful twisting feeling inside her, like being wrenched in two. That night Micky wet the bed. Auntie Jackie was furious. She had to wash his sheets in the canal.

"Some bloomin' holiday this is! Working my fingers to the bone washing and cooking all day, and nothing to look at but bloomin' cows!"

"I want to go home!" Micky said.

"Yes, and so do I!" Auntie Jackie bawled at him.

Micky began to scream. Milly sat white-faced and miserable.

"For heaven's sake, stop him!" Auntie Jackie shouted.

Milly climbed out on deck and went and sat by herself in the bow. The little boat was chugging happily along through a tunnel of sun-shot trees. Uncles Kevin and Kit were exchanging cross remarks in the cockpit and Micky's screams echoed through the woods like the calling of some mythical bird with outstretched talons come to take newborn babies from their cots.

Uncle Kevin came anxiously up the deck to Milly.

"You must stop him! What does he want?"

"He wants to go home."

"Do something about it!"

Milly went below to Micky and said, "We'll go home. Be quiet."

He stopped instantly.

"When?"

"Tonight," Milly said. She wanted it too, desperately. "When they're all in bed, we'll go."

He smiled.

Milly went back on deck and saw that they were coming to another lock. She was not sure what she had decided, but the thought of getting away from these bickering grown-ups, away on their own, was very attractive. After all, they only had to follow the canal. Home was at the end of it, across the sea. She had faced worse problems in her time. Tonight she and Micky would go home.

Three

In the evening they moored for the night near a road bridge. There was a sign on the bridge giving the name of a place three kilometers away, which Uncle Kevin said was not too far to walk to.

"We'll take you girls out for a drink after supper, how about that?" he said to Aunties Jackie and Marilyn.

"What about the children?"

"Oh, they'll be all right. Used to being left, aren't you?"

"We don't mind," Milly said.

"We'll see you into bed first," Auntie Jackie said. "And then we'll only be gone an hour or so. Just up the road."

When they had gone Micky said, "Now we're going home?"

"Yes."

Although the little boat was peaceful and friendly when they had it to themselves, there was this driving urge in Milly, once aroused, that was determined to go home. She wanted her mother and so did Micky. There would be no problems, she felt. All they had to do was just follow the canal, go back the way they had come. Walking hard, it would only take a few days to reach the sea, where the ferries sailed back to England.

"You've got to be good and do as I say," she said sternly to Micky. "We mustn't be seen, because they'll probably look for us, and you've got to walk all the time, quickly, not dawdle."

"Yes," he said.

"We'll take a few things."

The purse that the grown-ups called the kitty purse, for buying food, was in a drawer in the galley. Milly took five notes but she wasn't quite sure how much that was as money was different in France. Inside the purse she put a note saying, "I took 5, Milly." She did not want to be accused of stealing. She did not know if she would ever be able to pay it back, so perhaps it was stealing in a way, but if you said, she thought, it did not count. They would not have the two of them to feed any more, so perhaps it would work out equally.

She put a few things in a plastic carrier: a box of matches, some bread and cheese, a plastic mug, their toothbrushes and a washcloth. They would have to take a blanket each off their bunks for nighttime. She put these in two more plastic bags, which luckily Auntie Jackie collected, and gave one to Micky to carry. She made him put a spare sweater on top in case he got wet. He was wearing a teeshirt, shorts and sandals, and a sweater already. She had jeans and a teeshirt and a cardigan. She added a comb, and a bottle of lemonade, which was heavy but would soon go. She could not think of anything else.

"Are you ready?"

Micky nodded.

Milly humped up their beds to make it look as if they were still in them, in case Auntie Jackie looked in when she came back, then they went on deck and climbed over onto the canal bank.

It was not completely dark, but dusky, and very still. Milly stood a moment, thinking about what they were doing. She was excited, and frightened a bit, but more excited than frightened. It was very easy, just to walk back the way they had come. They were good walkers. The canal smelled and the yellow flags along the banks gleamed in the dusk, full of the rustlings and plops and ripples she had become accustomed to. Uncle Kevin said there was no life in ruddy France, but he had not ever listened to the goings-on in the rushes, as Milly had. At night it sounded louder.

"We shall travel by night," Milly thought. "We shall be part of the goings-on. We shall sleep in the day."

In the day the rushes were quieter. They would

sleep in the hot fields, with the cows.

"Now come on," she said severely to Micky, "we've a long way to go."

They set off along the towpath. Their eyes became adjusted to the night and there were no difficulties: the path was a good one. The only sounds were little animal noises, rustles and ripples and patterings that were not frightening. Because he was going home Micky was quite glad to walk obediently along the towpath, trailing his plastic bag, but after an hour or two he began to whine a bit: "My legs hurt. . . . Will you carry my bag? I want a cup of tea."

"No. We must keep on, else Uncle Kevin will come and find us."

That kept him quiet for another hour.

Milly kept thinking of the castle she had glimpsed amongst the trees high up on the bank: she thought of it as beckoning to them; she

imagined it at night with its narrow turret windows shining out over the silent canal, and she
longed to be that far on the way. "We will visit
there," she determined. She could not pass it by
without seeing it more closely. It made England
feel a lot closer, to think of the castle as halfway.

But long before the night was over Milly knew she would have to find somewhere to hide and sleep. She was terribly tired and Micky kept falling over.

They passed a dark lock cottage, but a dog on a chain barked at them and made them run. The sudden din, the rattle of the chain, scared Milly with its unexpectedness. She had grown accustomed to the deep loneliness and emptiness of the countryside. Micky, startled too, began to cry, not with fright but with weariness.

Milly knew they must find somewhere to sleep, but all the fields were soaking wet with dew; if they stepped off the towpath the long grass swept their bare legs like cold, wet, dogs' tongues. But when they came to the next lockhouse, silent this time save for a murmuring of roosting hens in an apple tree, they found a wooden shed just off the road, housing a battered car. It was in an orchard, away from the house. It had an earth floor and was dusty, dry and beautifully lonely.

"This will do us very well."

As they were both so tired Milly did not think the hard floor would keep them awake. There was a pile of empty paper bags that she spread out at the end of the shed to lie on. It made her think of the vagrants in London who slept under the bridge at Charing Cross wrapped up in cardboard boxes, and then she thought, "We are vagrants now. We are homeless." But she felt exhilarated rather than frightened. Micky, wrapped in his blanket, was asleep instantly, far too tired to complain. Milly was going to stay awake to think things over and make plans, but this first plan went wrong in two minutes. She was asleep too.

She woke knowing that they were in trouble. Someone was coming. It was just dawn, pearly gray, cold; she was shivering. A man was whistling, his footsteps clumping on the track, approaching, coming to get his car. Milly was lying with Micky in front of the car, at the back of the garage, and was too frightened to move. But there was no way out anyway. Micky still slept. Milly rolled closer to him, protecting him, pulling her blanket over them both to hide. The footsteps came into the garage, very close, and Milly heard the car door open. The man must have been within touching distance. For a few moments there was complete silence, and Milly thought perhaps the man was looking at them, but she could not tell. Her heart was thumping; she thought he must hear it. It was suffocating her, as if it had grown six times bigger. What was the man doing? There was a squashing, squeaking noise: the man getting into the driving seat. The door slammed. The engine whirred and coughed and Micky woke up with a jerk of alarm.

"Hush! Keep still!"

Milly pulled him tightly to her, the blanket

slipping down so that she could see the car backing out of the garage. They lay completely in view, but the man's head was turned to look behind him, the way the car was going. If he looked to the front he was bound to see them. But the car retreated, turning around once it was out, and the man kept looking backward all the time, to miss the trees. And when he went forward he did not glance into the garage at all. The car bumped away down the track, spluttering and coughing, and Milly released Micky from her grasp and sat up, hugging her arms tightly around her knees to keep herself from shivering.

"I'm hungry," Micky said.

Milly could not speak, she was so shaken. But Micky did not seem to have noticed anything amiss. He sat up and groaned and complained.

"I ache. I'm cold. I'm hungry."

Practical concerns galvanized Milly into life.

"Come on, we've got to get to England. It's no good complaining. We'll go on a bit, away from this place, and then we'll have breakfast."

She was stiff too, from the hard floor, her body like a piece of wood. She folded the blankets and put them in the plastic bags. She felt uneasy and frightened at the prospect before them. She had meant to be awake and make plans, all ready for today, but they were walking again, back on the towpath. The sun was just beginning to come through the trees.

"Do you think they're looking for us?" Micky asked.

"They will as soon as they wake up."

Luckily they didn't get up very early. Milly thought when they found out they would tell the police. If she was going to do some shopping, she should do it as soon as possible before the police started looking for them. They ate the bread and finished the lemonade.

"The next road that crosses the canal, we'll go and look for some shops," she told Micky.

He cheered up at that.

"Can I have some candy?"

"We'll see."

In an hour they came to a bridge and a road, and a signpost that said the name of a place and a number 2.

"That's not far," she said to Micky. "Come on."

She was tired already and Micky was trailing behind. She was beginning to think it was a very long way, but they hadn't been gone twelve hours yet.

The village was very small and sleepy, only twenty minutes away. There were just a few old houses lining the street, and a bit of a bulge in the road with some children standing there, carrying schoolbooks, and some old ladies talking. Milly had a feeling they were all staring at her as she walked past with Micky. She looked at the ground, pretending she was thinking of something important, but the feeling of her heart having grown bigger came back, making her feel breathless. None of the buildings seemed to be shops. Peering in the doors, all she saw was rooms with people sitting around the breakfast table, or women washing floors. There was sometimes a smell of coffee, or fresh bread, which made her feel hungry. Soon they had walked right through the village, and there was no shop.

Milly stopped. Ahead was country, and cows. But a bus was coming towards them. It passed by and stopped at the bulge in the road where the children were waiting. The children all got on but the driver got down and lit a cigarette.

Milly, drawn by the bus, took Micky's hand and walked back slowly. She went to the front and looked to see where the bus was going. It said "Dinan."

"That's the place we started from," she said to Micky. "Where we went on board the boat the first night."

It had never occurred to her that there might be an easier way to get to England than walking. They could ride to Dinan! She had the money out of the kitty purse—she felt for it in her jeans pocket. It was all there, safe. They could sit in luxury and watch the countryside roll past the window, like proper travelers!

They climbed on board at the front where there was a little counter to pay the driver. The driver climbed in after them and edged around in his seat. Milly held the notes in her hand.

"Der," she said, in her best French. (That meant two.) "To Dinan." She pronounced it *Dee*non, remembering how Uncle Kevin had got it wrong with the taxi driver, saying Dienan, to rhyme with divan, and the taxi driver had laughed.

"Der," repeated the driver, and then a word that sounded like zonfon. Milly said, "We," firmly, which meant yes, although she had no idea what zonfon meant. She knew yes and no, one, two and three, and please and thank you.

To her great relief, all seemed to be in order. He took three of her five notes and gave her some coins back, along with two tickets, a cheerful smile and some more incomprehensible words that fortunately seemed to require no answer. Milly put the coins safely in her back pocket and folded the notes up and stuffed them in too, and walked down to the back of the bus after Micky, wishing he had sat in the front seat because she hated everyone staring. She sat down and looked out of the window, feeling hot and red and thumping inside, and in the reflection from the glass she saw that her hair was all uncombed and had some straw sticking in it, and she had a smear of dirt down her cheek. The schoolchildren were all shiny and clean and were looking at her, pretending not to, and sniggering.

She felt much relieved when the driver started up the engine and they set off. Micky was looking out of the window, and his English remarks could not be heard by any of the curious, and it was lovely to see how fast the countryside bowled past compared with when they were walking. Although it was flat, she felt they were going downhill, freewheeling all the way. A deep content at her cleverness filled her whole body, and she lay back against the seat, smiling into the sunshine.

Four

All the schoolchildren got off after a few stops, and some shopping ladies got on and came and sat at the back. One elderly, fat lady sat down in the seat in front of them. She smiled at them and said something to Micky. He stared at her. Luckily the bus then started off. It went a few hundred yards and stopped again at the far end of the village. Two men in uniform were standing talking, and there was an official car parked. Milly knew they were *gendarmes*—French policemen— but they took no notice of the bus. When the bus set off again, it crossed a bridge, and over the parapet Milly saw the familiar canal, the still green water shaded by an archway of trees.

Micky said, "Perhaps those policemen were looking for us."

His tone of voice was merely conversational, not worried. The woman in front of them turned around and gave them a surprised look—Milly supposed not because of what Micky had said, but because he had spoken in a foreign language. She sank down in her seat, the lovely optimism fading into uncertainty.

The bus sped on through lush grassy fields and flowering hedgerows, and the woman in front of them kept turning around and staring at them. Micky had his nose pressed to the window and Milly shut her eyes and pretended to go to sleep, so that the woman would not talk to her. But her heart was thumping again. Fortunately there did not seem to be any more villages for some time, and the fat woman looked out the window too, and presently got out some knitting. Milly began to feel better. The fat cows in the long grass, so sleepy and content, were calming to the mind, like goldfish at the dentist's office, and the morning sun was getting very warm, flickering through the trees that shaded the road.

Then everything happened at once.

Micky said, "There's the canal again."

The bus was slowing down to cross a narrow bridge, and Milly saw a trim lockhouse and the water running down through the sluices into a lock, the canal beyond curving away like a green snake through the fields.

At Micky's remark, the woman turned around and said something to them, a question by the sound of it. Milly felt herself going red, not knowing what to say. She looked out the window, embarrassed, and saw that the bus was running into another village. There was a square ahead of them, and several people standing waiting, and just beyond the bus stop, three more *gendarmes*.

The bus came to a standstill. The doors opened. One of the *gendarmes* came towards the entrance door. While everyone was getting out of the back door, the *gendarme* stepped up into the front of the bus and asked the driver something. The fat woman got up and went to join in the conversation. Milly grabbed Micky by the hand and jerked him to his seat.

"I think they *are* looking for us," she hissed at him. "Come quickly."

She hustled him out through the back door and as she went down the step she saw the fat woman pointing to them, and the *gendarme* staring. She took Micky's hand and started to walk back along the pavement the way they had come, pretending to be ordinary, not hurrying. She had an instinct to get back to the canal, and her instinct was telling her to run like the wind, but her reason was telling her not to look as if she was in the wrong. They came to the canal and some stone steps that led down onto the towpath.

"Down here!" she hissed to Micky.

She could not resist looking back. All the *gendarmes* were staring after them. As she turned her head, one of them raised his arm and shouted after her.

"Run!" she said to Micky.

They leaped down the steps and onto the towpath, and Milly turned in the direction of England, grabbed Micky's hand again, and tore off as fast as she could. She was really frightened and desperate not to be caught now that they had come such a lovely long way on the bus, but she knew that in a few moments the policemen would be looking over the parapet of the bridge. The canal ran straight, heavily wooded on either side with the great canopy of shimmering leaves shading out the sunlight and dappling the path. Just at the very moment Milly guessed the *gendarmes*

would come to the parapet she darted sideways into the undergrowth. Micky crashed after her, and after a few moments' frantic passage through brambles and stinging nettles and dogwood and willow sedge, they burst through into the edge of a cornfield. The corn was well-grown, just turning yellow. Milly got down on her hands and knees and started to wriggle through it, making sure Micky was right behind her. She wriggled a good way into the field, twisting and turning every few yards, and then stopped, lying on her stomach. Micky was still coming, looking very surprised.

"Lie still," Milly whispered. "Still as a mouse!"

"Are they coming?"

"I hope not."

"I'm hungry."

"Yes, so am I."

She was not surprised that the police were looking for them. If they did not find them now, she felt quite optimistic, because she kept thinking what a lovely long way they had come in the bus. It felt like two days' walkings-worth, at least.

"I want to go home," Micky said. "I don't want to go back."

"Ssh. No. We won't."

She could hear the men talking on the towpath. They crashed about a bit in the undergrowth, and one of them came out onto the edge of the cornfield and gazed over the landscape. Milly and Micky lay still, silent.

Luckily the man had not come out in the same place as they had, so he never saw the telltale crushing of the corn where they had crawled. He stood and muttered and swore, and then crashed back through the brambles and undergrowth and shouted to the other men. After a little while they all left. Milly heard car doors slam on the bridge, and they drove away.

She sat up. It was very quiet and beautiful, the sun shining on the corn and the birds singing. She felt well-pleased and led the way back to the canal and the now-friendly towpath, deserted and cool under the trees.

"But they know we are here," she said to Micky. "They might come back or be waiting at the next bridge. We must be very careful." She added, "It's like a film on TV. We are being hunted. You must remember not to be seen."

Micky perked up at that.

"If we had a gun we could shoot them."

"No. That's wicked. They want to help us really, I suppose."

"You mean send us to England?"

"No." She thought that was unlikely. They would no doubt be delivered back to Uncles Kevin and Kit and Aunties Jackie and Marilyn, who would be frightfully bad tempered about it all.

"No," she said. "We'll only get to England on our own. So we mustn't let them find us. You must be very brave and determined."

Micky was brave and determined for about half
an hour. Then he said he was hungry.

"Yes, so am I, but I can't help it."

It was a nuisance there had been no shop before
they had got on the bus. It was very hot and they
were thirsty. Micky wanted to drink the canal
water but Milly wouldn't let him. The lockhouses
had faucets outside, but she knew they must not
be seen by any of the lock keepers. When they
came to a lock, they went off the towpath into the

fields and walked around it, and if there was a
lane to cross they lay in the hedge and made sure
it was clear before they passed it. At the third lock
the *gendarmes* were there, talking to the lock lady.
Milly and Micky hid behind a little woodshed,
waiting to see what would happen. They were glad
to have a chance to rest. It was very hot, and they
were sweaty and tired. The dropping of the canal
water through the sluice gates, cool and echoing
under the stone walls, made them feel thirstier
than ever. Milly found she was picturing the dank
wet walls of the inside of the lock, with the little
ferns growing out of the cracks.

The *gendarmes* and the lock lady were all

having a laugh together, not working hard at all. The *gendarmes* had put their hats on the lock gates and the lock lady brought out a tray of glasses and a bottle of wine for them. Then she brought them some pears on a plate.

Milly and Micky watched, silent and miserable. It was too awful to watch. Milly gave Micky a nudge and they slipped down the bank into the lane that approached the lock and crossed over. In a gateway on the far side the *gendarmes'* van was parked. They passed it to get through the gateway, and Milly saw a pack of chewing gum lying on the dashboard. She put her hand through the open window and took it, and pushed Micky on through the gateway and into an orchard. There were hens pecking about and Milly thought there might be some eggs, but she could not see any. The apples were not ripe yet, although she took a couple in passing. They did not come off very easily. They crawled through a hedge, through a field of weeds and poppies and eventually, when Milly decided it was safe, back onto the towpath again. Far in the distance they could hear the *gendarmes* talking and laughing. A faint smell of French cigarettes touched the warm air, and cool plopping noises came out of the canal where the fish were rising.

"Here." Milly opened the chewing gum and gave Micky a piece and one of the apples. The apples were hard and very sour, but the sharpness was refreshing. Milly craved a drink. She kept

thinking of great jugs of lemonade with ice cubes
floating in them, like advertisements. The midges
were biting, and Micky was having a hard time
being brave and determined, she could see.

She knew they must find some water to drink.
When they came to the next field of cows, she
thought the cows must have water to drink. They
did not drink from the canal. They crossed over a
dry ditch into the field and walked up to a row of
trees and bushes away from the canal, looking for
a pond or a water trough. At the far end of the
field there seemed to be a farmyard, for there
were old stone walls and roofs, and a haystack and
a gateway leading through. By the gate there was a
trough.

"There might be someone in the yard." They
approached cautiously, but it was very quiet, only
the swishing of the cows' tails and some pigeons in
the trees by the canal. The heat was very tiring;
she longed to sit down and have a rest.

Micky was starting to whine.

"Pretend we're in the desert, and we're looking
for a water hole," she said. "I think that's an oasis,
at the top of the field. But we must make sure the
enemy isn't hiding there."

It was very hard to make a game of it, but Micky
soon cheered up and started walking like a hero
again.

The trough was full of green dirty water. But it
had a pipe leading to it, and a round sort of

football floating on the surface. When you pressed the ball down, water gushed into the trough from somewhere underneath a metal flap at one end. By a lot of poking and fiddling about Milly found that if Micky held the ball down, she could cup her hands and catch clean water out of the pipe before it fell into the dirty green trough.

"It works like a tank on a toilet," she said.

"Is the water all right to drink, then?" Mickey said dubiously.

"Yes. It's all right. Here, your turn."

She held the orange ball down for Micky and he managed to get a good—if slow—drink. Then she had another turn. It was delicious. They stood with the cold water running down their chins, looking at the sleepy hot fields. Nothing moved save the cows' tails. The sky was burning blue and the distance all shimmering with the heat. Milly crossed over to the shade of the trees and said, "We'll have a little rest. We'll feel better afterwards."

Micky did not complain but lay down beside her. She could hear his empty tummy rumbling. She was worried about feeding him and tried to think of a solution to the problem, but her thoughts wavered off in other directions and then into nothingness.

Five

"**I**'m hungry," Micky said.

When Milly heard him and opened her eyes, she realized that it was some time later. The sun was still as hot, but the shadows were longer, and her body was stiff from lying down. Micky's arms were flung out in the grass, a dewdrop of sweat on his upper lip. He looked very frail to Milly, all her own responsibility, and she knew he needed feeding badly, and the day was ending and they would have to find somewhere for the night. For a moment she was very afraid; she felt like crying, her lips twitching with foreboding. It was very quiet and lonely. Even the cows had disappeared.

She gave Micky a little shake.

"Come on. We've got to walk on now."

Her voice came out better than she had feared, quite normal and sensible, and Micky seemed to take it for granted that he must get up and walk back to the canal, for he did not complain or ask any questions. They had a drink first, and set off. They came down to the familiar towpath and walked along, batting at the midges, kicking stones, trailing their plastic bags with the blankets in them. Milly knew that if the *gendarmes* appeared, she would have no energy now to run away.

The canal seemed to be running toward a slight hill, the land rising to their left and falling away on the other side of the canal to their right. The left bank was wooded and gradually grew steeper. They came around a long bend, and high up in the sky above the trees Milly suddenly saw a dazzling light, a reflection of the sun. It was a window winking up there, and the window was in the turret of the building that she had thought was an enchanted castle when they had passed it in the boat. She stopped and stared.

"Let's go there," she said to Micky.

She was so tired and hungry now that she knew they could not continue much farther.

"They might give us some food," she said hopefully.

After all, it was only the *gendarmes* who were chasing them. Other people could well be kind.

The bank steepened and grew into almost a cliff, with craggy boulders hoisting up through the trees and bushes. It was hard to find a good place to climb up for there was no path and neither of them had any strength left. Milly could feel her knees trembling, although she went on pretending to Micky that there was nothing wrong. The blanket bags were impossible, for they needed both hands to pull themselves up, so they left them behind to collect later. Milly still had the money, which was the only thing that seemed as if it might be useful. She got behind Micky and pushed him along ahead of her, and nagged him, and found the best way, but it was exhausting, and when they came to the top they found they could not even stand up, only pull themselves over the last crumbling ledge of the bank into a jungle of old rhododendron bushes and lie panting with the effort.

Milly had never felt so hungry in all her life, nor so sweaty nor so exhausted. She was frightened of her responsibility for Micky, who lay like a little white stranded fish on the bank. Nothing the castle had to offer could be worse than lying under the rhododendrons dying of exhaustion, so she started to crawl toward the gleams of sunshine she could see filtering through from some airy space beyond. She crawled like a dying snail until her face came into the sun.

They were on the edge of a lawn, mowed to green velvet, and the velvet unrolled to the walls of a tall gray stone house which stood magnificently on the brow of the wooded bank. On each corner of the house was a round turret with pointed windows and slate-shingled roofs like trout skins glittering in the thick gold evening light. Big windows and glass doors opened onto the lawn, and there were deck chairs scattered about and a table with some glasses on it. There was nobody about, and nothing moved, not a sound save the birds singing.

Micky saw the glasses on the table and said, "I'm going to have a drink," and got up and walked across the lawn.

Milly followed. There was nothing else to do.

The glasses were empty but there was a big jug like the advertisements Milly had been dreaming about earlier, half-full of a cloudy liquid with sliced lemons floating on the top. Micky drank straight out of the jug, down and down, until Milly could bear to watch him no longer and took it from him and did the same. She could feel it going down right into her very inside, icy-cold, because there were the remains of ice cubes floating in it. Micky took out the lemon slices and put them in his mouth, and looked towards the house.

"It's nice here," he said.

He was not afraid, but Milly was—although she was no longer sure what of. Getting to England was a far harder thing than she had imagined; they had done very well so far, but food and a rest were now more important than anything.

"Let's look in," Micky said.

"We shouldn't."

"Just look through the door."

He walked across the grass to the big windows and stood on the threshold. Milly hesitated, then followed him. She stood by him and looked.

The room was huge, stone-flagged, sparsely but elegantly furnished. In the middle of it was a large old-fashioned table with chairs pulled up to it. It was spread with a white cloth and a meal was laid out ready to eat. There was a large crusty loaf of bread and a dish of butter, a plate with fat slices of ham and chicken, a bowl of tomatoes and spring onions, a big quiche of eggs and leeks, baked gold, potatoes sliced and sprinkled with parsley in a white bowl, a big jug of cream, a dish piled with strawberries, and another full of trifle topped with cherries. They just stood and looked. Nothing moved in the house, and long shutters were closed to keep out the evening sun.

Micky moved forward and stood by the ham. Milly could see the expression on his face, his nostrils dilated to the smell, the look in his eyes. He looked at her.

"Yes," she said.

She walked to the table and cut off two slices of bread. They sat down and put the food on the plates, silently, quickly, eyes gleaming. The table was set for ten. Milly cut the quiche and lifted the slices with a knife. Micky took a pile of chicken, his favorite. They ate without talking, heads down.

Micky put butter thick on his bread and stuck strawberries in it and ate it with ham and tomatoes. And trifle, and then chicken again. Milly ate in the proper order, but very fast. When she had finished she saw that Micky was slowing down over his third bowl of trifle, his eyelids drooping and the spoon quavering, dropping blobs of jelly on the cloth. The beautiful table looked somewhat disarrayed, she noticed—plundered, to be exact, everything broken into and scattered.

She sat back, breathless with eating and worry. Micky, she felt sure, would never get across the green lawn, let alone down that difficult bank back to the canal, and she too . . . she could no longer think straight. Just as the lovely table spread with food had appeared before them as if by magic, she felt that somewhere there was a bed in a shuttered room, quiet and cool. She got up from the table and pulled Micky with her. They went out through a door into a great hall and up a wide curving staircase to the landing above. Milly looked into each of the rooms that opened onto the landing, and although they all had beds in them they looked as if people owned them and were likely to sleep in them that night, full of untidy clothes and sneakers and tennis rackets. She explored a small corridor and opened a door at the end. The door gave into a room that was perfectly round, empty save for a four-poster bed. The bed was made up, covered with a fluffy quilt patterned with rosebuds, but there were no possessions in the room, nothing save the bed, not even a chair.

Milly shut the door behind them and they both got into bed without taking anything off. The mattress and pillows were soft, engulfing them in a scent of starch and clean washing. It was like sinking into a cloud.

"It's like the Three Bears," Micky said and went to sleep instantly.

Milly smiled—it was true. She was too tired to feel frightened any more. She slept.

Six

They were awakened by sounds of pandemonium from below, muffled through the doors. They lay still, frightened. It was dark, warm; lights splashed out across the velvet lawns; car engines revved and scrunched on gravel, doors slammed, many voices were raised in a great uproar. Feet thudded up and down the stairs.

"Is it because of us?" Micky whispered.

Milly supposed so.

"Are we burglars?"

"Not exactly."

It was hard not to feel like it though.

Some of the voices were children's voices, shrieking, laughing, highly excited. They came down the corridors, opening doors and shouting. Somebody opened the door of the round bedroom and looked in. Milly and Micky were lying flat under the big fluffy quilt, which was pulled up over their heads, and no part of them showed. They heard the excited voices calling, somebody ran to the window and looked out, clattery shoes over the wooden floor. The language was incomprehensible but the gist of it was fairly clear. They all went out but left the door open. Milly peered cautiously out. The light came in from the landing to meet the moonlight coming through the window. How strange, Milly thought! She did not know what she felt, too tired to be frightened, too worried to move, too comfortable to care. She thought that, when all the fuss had died down and everyone had gone to bed, they could sleep again and then get up early and continue on their way, before the household got up. And stock up with food on the way out. Micky was already drifting into sleep again.

The house started to calm down a bit, not so many doors slamming and the voices not so clamorous. Milly turned over to sleep again but suddenly heard a scuffling on the floor, and felt something cold and wet against her face. She gave a great leap of fright and opened her eyes to see a large furry dog gazing into her face. Its amber eyes glinted in the half-light and a great pink tongue lolled out like a slice of the ham they had so much enjoyed a few hours previously. The dog whined and put up a paw playfully. Its tail was wagging with such pleasure that its whole back end went with it.

"Go away!" Milly said sternly.

The dog went as far as the door and then came back again, prancing and shaking its head. It got the edge of the quilt in its mouth and shook it, pulling it half off. Milly grabbed it.

"Go away!"

She put out a hand to bat the dog on the head but the dog thought she wanted to play and got hold of the quilt again. Milly pulled it back, and the dog barked.

Milly lay still, sweating.

Someone called from below.

The dog barked twice more at Milly, to play. It put its forelegs on the bed and stood trying to lick her face, while she pulled the quilt up and held it over her head.

"What is it?" Micky asked sleepily.

"Lie still and keep quiet."

She hoped if they were very still and all covered up the dog would get bored and go away, but it kept pulling the quilt. Every time she pulled it back the dog got another mouthful, thinking she was playing. Milly began to get desperate.

She put out her head and said, "Go!" in a very stern, quiet voice.

"It doesn't know English," Micky said.

The dog barked.

Voices were coming along the corridor calling the dog's name, which sounded like Shoe-Shoe. Shoe-Shoe gamboled to the door and stood there barking. Then it gamboled back again and pulled the quilt off the bed just as several people came into the room.

Someone put the light on. Then they all started gabbling, four almost grown-up children, two boys and two girls, all very brown and sporty-looking, in very short shorts and bright-colored teeshirts. The dog went on barking and Milly and Micky lay still and stared. Milly could not understand a word. One of the boys went to the door and called and presently two adults arrived and made great, amazed noises on seeing Milly and Micky. Milly could see that they did not know whether to be cross, indignant, curious or helpful. They kept asking questions but none of it made sense. The word zonfon occurred again, and the woman bent down and said something into Milly's face, as if she were an idiot.

"Voo zett lay zonfon zarnglay?" is what it sounded like.

"Eel zon tarnglay," said one of the youths and stood over them and said, "You are English, yes?"

"No," Milly said. After that, whatever they said, in bad English or in gabble, she would not answer.

Somehow, in spite of the noise, she found it hard to keep awake, still lying in the bed, and Micky, in fact, dozed off again. Not much was forthcoming in English, but she supposed that they had been reported missing and that these people realized that they had found the missing persons. But it was late, and with luck they would not call the police until the morning. Gradually, they all withdrew, yawning, the excitement over. The lady pulled the quilt up and said something that sounded kindly, and patted Micky's cheek. She was the last to leave. She put the light out and shut the door. Listening very carefully, Milly heard the key turn in the lock. To make sure, she got out of bed and tried the door handle. Yes, the door was locked.

Milly got back into bed, scowling. Before the door was locked, she had felt soothed and fairly resigned to being caught and taken to the police, but with the turning of the key she felt quite the opposite: stubbornly determined to continue on their journey. Perverse was the word her mother would have used. She decided to go to sleep now, and wake very early and work out what was to be done before anyone else was awake. They had come so far, with such a mixture of luck, guile and suffering, that it seemed dreadful to waste it. She had got used to the feel of it: the initial jumpiness, the nervous sweat, had given way to a sense of using the basking empty countryside as a cover, like a wild animal. The domesticity of the flowery bed was welcome for a few hours, but after that . . . Milly scowled, and fell asleep scowling.

Seven

She awoke when it was just beginning to get light.

Everything was different now, except the resolve to get on with the journey. The house was silent. Milly slipped out of bed and went first to the door, which she found was quite definitely locked, and then to the window, the only other way out. The view was over the tops of trees to a misty horizon far away, faint and blue as far as the eye could see, and between the treetops and the horizon lay miles of blurred meadows and slumbering farms and coils of mist lying over the canal like cobwebs. It was all cold and still and glittery with damp. The window was tall and narrow and had no useful balcony or drainpipe, nothing below it save the smooth stone wall of the turret plummeting down to the grass below.

Milly, looking out, thought of the princess in the story who let down her hair for the prince to climb up. But her hair was short as a brush and even the princess could not have climbed down her own hair. Climbing down was the only way out, so she considered it.

Although the turret window had such a breathtaking view over the treetops, it was not actually as high off the ground as the panorama made one think, for the trees were rooted in the steep bank that fell to the canal, far below the level of the lawns. The bedroom was only on the next floor up from the ground. When she looked up, Milly saw that the turret went up quite a long way above, so their problem was not as difficult as it might have been. Which was encouraging in theory, but in practice not a great help.

In films about fires in hotel bedrooms people cut the sheets in strips and tied them together and let themselves down. Milly went back to the bed and looked at the sheets. There was the quilt cover, which was so pretty, but she had nothing to cut it with. She stood looking at it. Micky woke up and she said, "I want to cut the sheets up but I haven't any scissors."

"I've got my penknife," Micky said.

He rummaged in the pocket of his shorts and brought it out. It was a tiny one his father had given him once, and Micky's great treasure, but Milly had forgotten all about it. She took it, opening the blade, and considered the quilt anxiously. Cutting the quilt seemed to her quite awful, far worse than eating the food last night or taking the chewing gum. It was exquisitely pretty and expensive looking.

Then she thought of her resolve and determination. Cutting the quilt was not *hurting* anybody. These people looked very rich and could easily buy another. She took a big breath, frowned resolutely, and undid the quilt from the eiderdown inside it. She pushed the little blade through the material and made a hole, and pulled. It seemed to make a very loud noise, tearing the material. The strips had to be wide enough to be strong, but narrow enough so that there would be enough of them to reach the ground, no easy compromise. The knots took up quite a lot too. It wasn't an easy task, not like in films at all. It seemed to take hours. She kept hanging the quilt-rope out the window to see if it was long enough to reach the ground. But when she thought of the alternative to what she was doing—lying in bed waiting for Monsieur and Madame to unlock the door and take them back to Uncle Kevin and Auntie Jackie way back in the inside of France—she was encouraged and hacked on.

When it was ready she tied the end to the bar between the two narrow windows. There was only just room to squeeze through, and she did not know whether her knots were good enough. Her mother had always called her a worrier. Her mother wasn't a worrier at all, only about their father. And he was enough to drive a woman insane, the neighbors said, and her mother wasn't insane at all. Only tired. Milly longed for her mother. Sitting on the windowsill, full of worries, it was the thought of getting back to her mother that made her overcome all the dreadful doubts.

Micky would have to go first. She got down and got him to climb over the sill. She lowered him down till he got his hands on the quilt-rope and was dangling against the wall.

"Wrap your legs around it, like in the gym," she said.

"I can walk down the wall," he said, pushing his feet against the stone.

Milly watched one of the knots slither tight and trembled over the windowsill. She was petrified for Micky, who was dependent upon her handi-work, but he was enjoying himself.

"Ssh!" she hissed, remembering the dog. "You mustn't make a sound. Go on, stop fooling around!"

She was in agony, seeing him lurch and slither and giggle down the wall. For herself, there was no fear at all, only the need to hurry and join him. As soon as he was down, she flung herself out, grazing knees and knuckles, flailing wildly, sick with hurry. She slid down scarcely in control, burning her hands, bumping agonizingly against the stone.

"You're rotten at it," Micky said.

"Hush! Quick! Sssh!"

They ran. Milly was all pains and panics, tearing across the lawn. When she looked back she saw that they had made long trails in the dew, so she made Micky follow her back the other way, away from the canal, in case anyone followed, until they got to a belt of trees. Then she thought by the time the excitable family got up the sun would have dried the trails. It was still only just morning, in spite of the time she had taken with the rope, a damp, blurry imminence of day, the first birds beginning to sing, the first tentative shivers of light spreading across the cold sky. In the cover of the trees, confidence returned. Milly led the way, keeping to the edge. The front of the castle was grazed by cows and bounded on both sides by trees, with a gravel drive down the middle. Looking back, seeing the white thread of her rope dangling from the tower, Milly could not believe that it was not a fairytale place, and the rope for a prince, the tower for a princess. She paused a moment, to remember it, but the exulting, enormous splendor of having escaped so cleverly suddenly burst in her like a horse chestnut splitting its spiny jacket in autumn, and she laughed out loud. She really was *clever*! Bold and cunning and invincible.

"It's good, eh?" she said cheerily to Micky. "We fooled them, didn't we? I bet they'll sleep for ages yet."

"My knife was good."

"Yes. Poor old quilt."

There was a lane at the end of the drive. Milly boldly turned away from the canal, towards a village. They would get a bus and go to Dinan; the *gendarmes* would be searching along the canal. She remembered their bags of luggage abandoned on the cliff, but did not care. They would not need them anymore. They were nearly back to the sea, and she still had money. She walked boldly, and Micky followed her, pleased with having climbed out of the tower.

Eight

Walking was such a terribly slow method of travel for someone in a hurry. They came to a village and it was still asleep and there was a signpost saying Dinan 15. The 15 meant kilometers, which was shorter than miles, Milly remembered, but she could not remember by how much. Things were irritatingly different in France.

This time there were no buses and nobody about, and no shops again, either open or closed, only a straggle of whitewashed houses. Outside one of the houses, leaning against the wall, was a bicycle. It was run-down and old-fashioned, and had a child's seat on the back. Milly noticed it as they walked past, and then kept thinking about it as they walked on out of the village and into the country. After a bit they came to a gateway into a field and Milly leaned on the gate, still thinking. Micky said he was hungry and Milly said, "Wait here."

It wasn't stealing, she kept telling herself, only borrowing. Nobody could call it stealing. She walked back into the village and past the bicycle, not stopping. Then she turned around and walked back more slowly, approaching the bicycle as if she was stalking it, very quietly. Not to frighten it, she thought. Only *she* was frightened, her heart doing its crashing act against her ribs again, so fast and loud she felt sick. She came up to the bike and put her hands on the handlebars and walked on with it, scarcely breaking her stride. She pushed it out into the road and got on it, hopping and wobbling and sweating with fright. She had half expected alarm bells to go off, dogs to bark, church bells to peal out, but nothing happened at all, save the whirring and clattering of the bike itself and her own gasps and grunts to get it going. It was heavy and old-fashioned and needed a lot of leg pushing. But once going, it moved majestically, like a double-decker bus, and as she passed out of the village, Milly's fright gave way once more to a great soaring of triumph and delight. She pushed faster and faster on the pedals until she had no breath, and the bike hummed over the pavement as if as anxious to get to Dinan as she was.

When she got to the gateway, Micky was sitting on the top bar.

"Wow!" he said, admiringly.

75

"Get on then."

She stopped with a grinding of brakes, wrestling with the great handlebars. She gave Micky a pedal to get on by.

"Hang on!"

They staggered into movement, lurching across the road. Milly fought for control, pilot of a wartime bomber, she was thinking, the ponderous machine with Micky on board (a full load of bombs) almost more than she had the strength to cope with. But, obligingly, the road dipped downhill and they gathered speed. She sat back on the seat and gazed hopefully ahead, and for a few minutes the countryside went past effortlessly, just like through the bus window. There was a slight bend coming, and Milly could hear a car. As they came into the bend, she discovered to her horror that the car coming towards them was on the wrong side of the road. It hooted furiously and swerved to avoid them, and the driver put his head out and shouted a tirade of very rude-sounding language.

Micky turned around and put his tongue out.

"Pig," Milly said. "French pig."

But after it had happened twice more she began to worry. The drivers all shouted at her and hooted. Perhaps they recognized the bicycle, she thought, and were on their way to tell the owner it had been abducted. But why did they all drive on the wrong side of the road? Was it a French habit?

"I'll ride on the other side of the road," she said. The French had some strange ways, after all. They put bread with butter on it into their coffee and slurped it up very rudely, which, even in their lax household, would have been considered bad manners. But the French did it in cafés, smartly dressed. They did not put their knives and forks together when they had finished. They drove on the wrong side of the road.

She crossed the road, and after that it was all right. Nobody remarked upon them at all, and went past politely, giving them plenty of room, no hooting, no shouting.

Milly toiled on and Micky sang in his tuneless voice, saying at regular intervals, "Are we nearly there?" After a bit, thinking they must be, Milly said, "Yes," and then she remembered that Dinan was only the place where they had joined their little boat—the place they needed to get to was St. Malo, a long taxi-drive farther on. But when she felt herself feeling depressed by this, she remembered that it was only the night before last that they had set out. It seemed a century ago, but in fact it was only one whole day and a bit, which meant that they had made amazing progress. She had to keep telling herself this, over and over again, as her legs grew more and more tired, and her lungs grew sore and sweat ran down her face. It was getting hot again, and the leafy green lanes went on forever over the countryside of cows and long grass. How *boring* France was!

In spite of the bicycle, it took them nearly all day to reach Dinan. On the uphill bits they had to walk, Micky as well, and there seemed to be a lot of them, and they walked slower and slower. The bike was then very heavy to push, and in the end, when they came to quite a long hill, Milly had no strength left and pushed it into the hedge and left it. She knew they had not far to go, for they had seen the town in the distance through a gap in the hedge. They had managed to get a drink or two in water troughs but were getting ravenously hungry again.

"There will be shops, and we'll buy candy," Milly said.

They lay down to rest in some woods and fell asleep. When they awoke the sun was much lower in the sky and the shadows were growing longer. Milly had a feeling of panic. This time, she knew, there would be no enchanted castle and no table spread with delicious food. It would not happen twice. But Dinan was their destination. To get there would be an achievement, whatever happened afterwards.

The sun was very low behind the town when they came to its outskirts. They were high up and could see the river winding away below and the tall bridge crossing it on long stone legs like stilts, bringing the traffic into the gnarled-up tangle of streets on the hill. They could see the dark snake of the waterway they had set out along and could follow it through tangled gardens and fields back into the countryside that they had traveled through. In spite of her weariness, Milly was proud of what she had done, reaching Dinan without being caught. She felt like a pilgrim, footsore and exhausted, seeing her holy city in the rays of the setting sun. It wasn't the city she wanted . . . but the next one would be . . . and this was real enough for now. She thought of her mother and lifted her chin stubbornly. But she was tired, the panics were not far away, as she thought how to feed Micky, how to find someplace for the night. She had to be very firm with herself.

"Come on."

The town was all narrow, busy streets, big squares, stone ramparts overlooking the river, cobblestones and alleys in confusion. There were a lot of restaurants and tables outside, and the most delicious smells emanating from doorways. There were no scruffy children like themselves sitting at the tables, only well-dressed grown-ups and French families speaking their terrible gabble and tearing at lobster legs with their strong peasant teeth during lulls in the conversation. It was nothing like home at all. The foreignness of it dazzled Milly. She walked from delicious smell to delicious smell along the sidewalks, looking at the plates of food, pressing her nose to windows of sizzling steaks and joints on spits. She was dizzy with it, the hallucinations of food on every street corner. Micky was wailing in her wake.

"I'm hungry!"

People stared at them, half amused, too interested.

"Shut up," she said, "and I'll buy you something. Not a dinner, but something."

She wanted to save most of the money for traveling. Food for them must be plain. There was a baker still open with three loaves left, long as walking sticks. She bought one, offering up a coin hopefully and getting some smaller ones back. She tore the bread in half and gave half to Micky to shut him up. But the smells of roasting meat still made them feel weak.

Milly felt her legs failing. When she stood still they trembled. She stood still, just to feel them. It was dark now and everyone was going home. We must find a quiet place, she thought, before my legs give out. She walked from the busy streets into the quieter ones, through a big cobblestoned square. Being high on the brow of the cliff that swooped down to the river, the town had strange open places and steep walls with squares below, the levels unexpected. They looked over a parapet and saw a park below them. It was quiet and secret, the tops of the trees coming up to them. There was a children's zoo directly below where they were looking, a big corner fenced off with antelopes grazing in the dusk, alone after the day. There was a shed with piles of hay, and a lot of carrots, and buckets of water. Everything we need, Milly thought. She didn't think the antelopes would mind. The fence was of wire mesh, like around a tennis court, and if they climbed over the stone parapet the mesh came up to where their toes could reach it. It was a long way down, but nothing to daunt the intrepid escapers from castle turrets.

"You can do that, can't you?" she said to Micky.

"Sleep with them goats, you mean?"

"They're not goats, they're antelopes."

"Will they mind?"

"No."

She went first to prove her point. They watched her descent, but made no move, still grazing. Micky followed dubiously. They went into the little shed. It was warm after the sun of the day, the earth floor trodden hard, quite clean. Milly took some hay and made a bed. The antelopes didn't seem to mind. Micky and Milly ate some carrots and drank some water, and Milly found her legs had stopped trembling. Inside the shed was very comfortable and very private and warm enough so that they did not regret the blankets they had abandoned. The antelopes were perfectly friendly. One of them came in and ate some of the hay they were sitting on, its head very close, its large sloe eyes regarding them calmly. Milly could smell its herbal, musky smell. She lay with her eyes shut and listened to its neat little teeth chomping away, very steady. The lullaby noise soothed her, backed in the distance by the evening noise of towns, of car doors slamming, shouts and whistles, a distant train grinding and vibrating away into the country.

"What shall we do tomorrow?" Micky asked.

"We shall go to St. Malo and get on the ferry," Milly said.

"How?"

She didn't know.

"We shall go home tomorrow," she said.

She spoke very firmly, for it was important to believe it. This time tomorrow night, they could be on the ship going back to England. It would be no more amazing than what they had done already. She held fast to the idea and would not let any doubts in.

Nine

Milly had intended to wake early and make an escape before anyone was about, but she slept fitfully through the night and fell sound asleep just when she should have been waking up. When she did wake up, she was aware that things had gone wrong as soon as she opened her eyes.

Deserted as it had seemed last night, the park was now busy with people going to work, a little knot of whom were standing with their noses pressed to the wire, staring into the hut at the two new residents in the antelope pen. They were laughing and pointing and other people passing by stopped to see what the excitement was.

Milly sat up abruptly, horrified by her careless- ness. She gave Micky a great shake and he opened his eyes.

"We must get up," she said. "It's late." (For all the world as if they were at home and had missed the start of school.)

The keeper was coming along the path and the people in the crowd shouted to him and pointed.

"You mustn't say a word, and do as I say," Milly said. If they spoke, everyone would know they were English and the *gendarmes* would be called. But if they were quick and slippery, she thought they might be able to make a run for it.

"You must be ready to run. Very fast. We don't want to be caught."

"No. We've got to catch the boat."

She was frightened again, with all the now-familiar symptoms, breathless and tight in the chest with all her insides grown too big for her skin. She got hold of Micky's hand firmly and went out of the shed.

The keeper went to the gate with his key and the crowd drifted along curiously. Milly walked over to the gate sternly, although her legs were feeling as bad as the night before. To get outside was the first objective. The man opened the gate and con-fronted them, half laughing, like the crowd, half inquisitive. He was young and did not look put out, but everyone crowded around; there was no way through. They were all talking and asking ques-tions, and one woman stepped forward and bent down and asked Milly something, pushing her face into Milly's, a severe, fussy face, a do-gooder of the worst kind, Milly decided. She stared back in the way she had long ago discovered worked the best: blank, as if she were deaf. Even when she understood what they were saying she used this defense, and when she didn't understand, as now, it made it much easier. Blank, uncomprehending, holding tightly to Micky. When there was a chance, she intended to run for it.

Nobody was much bothered save one or two fusspots, especially the woman. Most of the people had to get on to work. The crowd thinned away. The woman straightened up and looked around and said something to the keeper. Milly heard the word "*gendarme*." The young keeper shrugged, grinned, and then turned away into the pen with a gesture that quite plainly meant he was going to get on with his work. Milly began to feel more hopeful.

The woman tossed her head and tutted, and put her hand on Milly's shoulder and gave her a little push to shepherd them along the path with her, making for the square. The others came with them because they were going that way, but the woman had taken over. She had her hand on the small of Milly's back, guiding her, but no firm hold. She had very high heels on, and was too old to be much good for chasing. She was talking in a very bossy voice to the others. Milly began to feel more optimistic, as long as there were no *gendarmes* in sight.

She gave Micky's hand a squeeze and whispered,

"Be ready to run for it. When I say. Don't say anything."

The woman, seeing her whispering, started jabbering at her again, sharp pointed sentences, questions no doubt. Milly gave her more blank stares. She was, after all, quite experienced in looking after herself against meddlers. She thought, with almost a smile, that if Micky started to scream, in the middle of the town, the bossy woman would soon leave them to themselves. But it was not what Milly wanted, to be noticed. To vanish, dissolve, disappear was her intention. The woman made them hurry, her heels clacking hard over the cobblestones. Milly kept her eyes peeled, thinking fast. They came to a busy road and crossed over, and on the other side there was another square, and a market in progress. There was a sidewalk bounding it, lined with trees, and the woman set off with them down the sidewalk, but the market was a more perfect haven than Milly could have conjured up in her most optimistic dreams. She had only to hold hard on to Micky and duck away sideways into the thick crowd, belting down an alleyway between vegetable stalls. She went very suddenly, practiced. The woman stopped and shouted after them but was not—as Milly had observed—a chasing lady. It was easier than Milly had dared hope. Winding expertly through the densest part of the crowd, she felt quite safe when she pulled up, still holding Micky.

Micky, looking about him, said, "I'm hungry."

Food winked and beckoned to them in every direction, stalls of cheeses and butter, of fresh, glittering fish and vegetables and salad stuff of every color and dew-fresh desirability. Milly groped in her back pocket and brought out the coins left over from the loaf of bread. She was determined to keep the rest for traveling, but the coins, offered hopefully at a candy stand, were rejected impatiently. The woman was horrid. When she turned to serve another customer, Milly took two toffees from a pile, left her smallest coin in their place, and walked on, peeling the paper off. She gave one to Micky.

"That's your breakfast. We can't waste time here."

She wanted to find a bus going to St. Malo, and decided to start walking out of the town following the directions to St. Malo and see what happened next. It was going to be hot again and she was tired already. But today—*today* . . . it was within reach now, given the same luck that had attended them faithfully so far. And in the crowded town, nobody noticed them as they did in the sleepy villages. Micky followed, scuffling his feet. He looked pale and weary, but did not complain, merely scowling and muttering to himself from time to time.

They came to the country quite soon but there was no sign of a bus. After a little while they came to a sign that said, "Camping," with an arrow pointing down a lane. As they were thirsty, Milly decided it was worth investigating. Camping must mean water, how could you camp without it? She turned into the lane and Micky followed.

At the bottom of the lane there was a clearing in some trees and quite a lot of trailers parked, attached to cars. Some of them had GB notices. One of them was small, bright red, and had a cage of parakeets in the window. Milly fastened her eyes on it, amazed. Several people were walking about, or sitting at their camping tables eating. There was a brick building, containing bathrooms, in the center of the site, and a little wooden office under the trees. There were quite a lot of children playing or wandering about, but nobody took any notice of Milly or Micky.

Milly could not take her eyes off the red trailer. Was it *meant* that they should come across it again? The garden gnomes were sitting in folding chairs, reading newspapers. The trailer door was open. They must be on their way home, Milly thought; they must be on their way to St. Malo. A smell of the British cooking their bacon drifted across the site.

"I'm hungry," Micky said.

"Yes." Milly was not thinking of food.

She walked slowly over toward the bathrooms, Micky following.

"We can have a drink."

There was a drinking fountain. Micky drank

fast, then Milly. All the time she was watching the red trailer. She went and stood outside the brick building, leaning against the wall, and made Micky stay with her. People came in and out, and some children came and bounced a ball against the wall. Micky yawned.

"Can't we go?"

"Not yet."

After about ten minutes the father gnome laid down his paper and said something to the mother gnome. They got up and smoothed their papers and put them in the car. They opened the trunk of the car and folded the chairs and put them in. Mother gnome picked up her handbag and they both came toward the bathrooms.

Milly made up her mind. She was becoming used to making momentous decisions, and this was the most momentous yet. If the trailer was empty, and tidy, and ready to go (which she guessed was the case) they would get in and hide. If it still had the breakfast things on the table it meant the gnomes would tidy it before they set off, which would be no good. As she walked toward it she thought, "It will be decided by how it is. I will do whatever seems right." By that reasoning she could pretend there was no decision to make.

As soon as the two elderly people had come past them and into the building, Milly went to the trailer and looked in. The inside was neat as a new pin, swept, everything folded and stowed. She looked back to the bathrooms. There were no

windows looking in their direction, so the gnomes
could not see them.

"Get in," she said to Micky.

He hopped up the step.

"Gosh," he said. "Will they take us?"

"Yes."

The decision started to go wrong at that moment. Inside the trailer there was nowhere to hide.
It was so small it was just one room, and all the

cupboards were stuffed full, and the closet too. Milly had just discovered that when she saw that the gnomes were coming back.

"Sit down," she said to Micky, "and sssshh!"

She sat down on the floor in the corner behind the door and squashed Micky with her. Micky's eyes were wide open now, astounded. Milly's fright symptoms were nearly bursting her, the little trailer seeming to thud and rock to the thumping of her fears.

They heard the gnomes talking.

"We've all day, there's no hurry."

"I'd like to look around the town before we go."

"Very well. We'll push off now then, and that will give us plenty of time."

The door swung to and closed, without anybody coming in. A key turned in the lock. Pause. Jerk. Car doors slamming. Engine coughing, whirring, jerk again. Very slowly the trailer started to move away. It swayed and creaked and things tapped and rolled in the drawers and cupboards and the bird cage rolled from side to side.

Milly and Micky got up very carefully and sat on the sofa thing under the window. They could scarcely believe their good luck. They pressed their noses to the window and saw the green lane rolling past them, which they had toiled up hungrily less than half an hour before. For one really terrible moment at the bottom, Milly thought the gnome was going to turn back to Dinan, the way they had

come, but no—all was well . . . he was only doing a
wide turn so that the trailer would not get hung up
on the corner. He turned left for St. Malo, and
the car gathered speed.

Milly could not help laughing out loud.

Micky said, "Those parakeets aren't real. They're
stuffed."

They examined them, rocking in their cage, and
it was quite true: they were fake parakeets, wired
to the perch, their bead eyes glittering. Milly
thought it very odd.

"Real ones would be sick," Micky said, watching
their feverish rocking. After a bit he said, "I'm
hungry."

Milly opened a few of the cupboard doors.
There was plenty of food: a little refrigerator with
butter and eggs, and a bread bin, and, under a lid,
a little stove. Milly had the brilliant idea of cooking
breakfast, but she could not get the stove to light,
so supposed it was turned off in some way she
could not fathom. Instead she got out the bread
and the butter dish, and found a pot of honey and
a jar of marmalade. They sat at the table and
stuffed, and watched the landscape flying past.
Sometimes they got views over a huge river, and
Milly remembered the taxi ride, and the glimpses
of the river in the moonlight. Now it basked in
sunshine, flecked with seagulls and the occasional
sailboat. Milly could see that it was growing wider
and wider, and at the end of it there would be the

93

sea and the ships sailing to England. She began to feel very excited, almost burning with the feeling. It was so close . . . and yet the hardest part of all was still ahead: to get on the boat without any tickets. Even to get out of the trailer was going to be tricky.

"We could stay on it, and go in the hold," Micky said.

But Milly thought the gnomes would come in for a meal before the day was out. Or perhaps they wouldn't. Perhaps there would be no decision to make, like earlier on. Perhaps there would be no choice. Thinking about it made her feel very fidgety. She felt burning hot and itchy and a bit sick. She longed, *longed* to be at peace on the big ship, sailing for England. After that, nothing would stop them, whatever happened.

The gnomes drove to St. Malo without stopping on the way. Milly felt sicker and sicker. She sat with her eyes shut, all screwed up for it to work out all right. At the beginning it hadn't mattered so much, somehow. But now they had come so far, nearly all the way, in fact, it mattered terribly not to get caught.

When she opened her eyes she could see that they were in a town, with traffic zooming past, and people peering in at them through the windows. They stopped at traffic lights, and she thought the best thing would be just to step out here, and run, but they were locked in. She examined the window.

It would open, but could never be got through in the time they would be stopped at a traffic light; it wasn't deep enough. If Micky got through, there would never be time for her, or vice versa. And people would be bound to stare, and the gnomes would notice. She got more and more itchy as they stopped and started through the traffic. The town was on the edge of the sea. They could not go much farther. They would fall in.

They came out onto a pier and drove along with the harbor on one side and a high wall on the other. There were a lot of cars parked along the wall, and when after a bit there was a big enough gap, Milly saw that they were going to park there too. As they came to a halt, she was so frightened she thought she was going to be sick. There was bread and knives and jam jars all over the table and crumbs all over the floor—nowhere to hide! If they came in . . .

"Get down here!" she hissed to Micky, pulling him behind the door. "Be ready to run if I say—if they come in—"

Her heart was banging, making her shake like jelly. The gnomes were old, she told herself, they wouldn't be able to catch them. She heard the car doors open, and slam shut. She held her breath. Micky wriggled. Voices, outside the door. Milly felt herself tingling, burning, like being suffocated, waiting for the sound of the key in the lock. More talking, laughing. Then nothing.

They waited. Nothing at all. Silence. Milly listened for ages and felt herself calming down, her breath coming back.

"They've gone away," Micky said.

They waited to make sure, then looked out again. It was true. There was nobody there, only the row of cars parked and a few people on bicycles, and tourists looking at the water, no sign of any gnomes at all.

Milly couldn't believe their luck.

She opened the window on the side nearest the wall and pushed it as wide as it would go.

"Come on, get out. I'll give you a leg up."

It was a dreadful squeeze, but fortunately nobody seemed to pay any attention to them. Milly shut the window behind them, noticed the food things all over the table, and wished she had cleared up. Whatever would the gnomes think? But it did not matter now. Now they had to find a boat and get on it. This was going to be the hardest part of all.

Ten

Finding the boat was not difficult.

It was there against a pier, as large as life. There was a Hovercraft thing, too, going to Jersey, and lots of British people milling about with luggage, and cars in long lines waiting to go in the boat's jaws, and buses full of people from Birmingham and schoolchildren on educational expeditions. But where you got on, at the bottom of a gang-plank, there was a man looking at everyone's tickets. Milly watched him for a bit, then went and looked at the cars driving on. They drove on without any trouble, and the people got out and walked away into the top of the boat up a staircase. If there had been a way of getting into somebody's car it would have been quite easy. Or one of the trailers. Their red trailer did not seem to be catching this boat, for it did not come to join the line, and Milly decided they had done the right thing in leaving it. But she longed to get in another one.

This was impossible, unless one asked. And Milly knew perfectly well that if she asked, nobody would say, "Yes, dear, of course. Do get in." They would say, "But where is your mummy and daddy, dear?" Even if she said, "In England, that's where we're going," people—being what they were (and she *knew* this, through bitter experience)—would be compelled to meddle, to ask questions, to do good. They never did what you wanted. It always had to be right, to comply with these laws of what children did do and what children did not do. And Milly knew that children of nine and six did not travel alone on steamers to foreign parts, nor home again either. "Although they *can*," she thought defiantly. "We have proved it." At least, almost. Nearly, right to the foot of the gangplank.

"And we *will*," she determined. "We will do it. We're not going to fail now."

She was trembly again, but this time it was not with weariness, nor fright, just determination. To get on board . . . once the boat had sailed, nothing would matter then, because it would not turn back to deliver them to Uncle Kevin and Auntie Jackie, however annoyed they might be. Boats did not do that sort of thing.

She needed to be very, very clever.

When the buses went on board, they were empty except for the driver. The passengers all got out and went up the gangplank in a bunch and only one person bothered to talk to the ticket man and show his papers. At first Milly waited by a bus door to see if they might manage to nip in when everyone had left, but as the door was just beside where the driver sat it did not look very hopeful. The drivers always had their heads turned that way, making jokes and helping the old ladies.

Micky could not take his eyes off the cars loading. He was not interested in anything else. Milly wanted to explore possibilities amongst the trailers in the line, but Micky did not want to come.

"You can stay here," she said, "by this post. We've got to get on the boat somehow, but you mustn't go away, whatever happens. I am going to see. I'll be back in a minute."

"I'll watch the cars."

"Yes."

Milly did not really know what she was looking for: some kind lady to scoop them up and say, "There, dears, of course I'll take you to England. Don't worry about a thing." But there were no kind ladies looking for needy children. Only impatient car drivers looking at their watches. The boat was due out in twenty minutes. Milly was beginning to feel panicky again, and desperate. If the boat went without them, after all they had achieved . . . to be left behind in *beastly* France . . . She felt the tears pricking. The boat let out a blast on its horn. A big bus full of schoolchildren coasted down the pier and pulled up at the end of the line. After that there was nothing. The schoolchildren were terribly well-looked-after, three or four teachers clucking around them like mother hens. Milly stared at them angrily. Lucky *pigs*! She wanted to say something to one of the teachers. She could *ask* them, perhaps, throw herself on their mercy. She could say their parents had already gone to England and left them behind because—because—she could not think why . . . even bad parents did not actually do such careless things. . . .

She went back to get Micky, the desperation mounting. She got to the post, and he wasn't there. He wasn't anywhere to be seen. She looked around scared, the panics rising fast. The big bus was just moving forward to go on board. After the bus there were only two more cars.

"Micky!"

This was awful, the very worst moment of the whole trip. The steamer let out a blast on its horn.

"Micky!" she screamed.

She gazed in despair at the great jaws of the steamer and the bus going into the hole that was left for it, right near the edge where the great door-flap was hinged. She looked up at the towering black sides and all the people happily crowded on the rails above, laughing and pleased to be going home, shouting, waving. One figure was waving wildly.

"Milly! Milly, I'm here!"

Micky! He was on board, laughing, waving, bunched up in the great crowd over her head. He was laughing with his cleverness at getting on board.

The last of the two cars was just going into the exact gap that was left, and as she watched, Milly saw a sailor make a signal for the doors to be closed. The panic burst out in Milly. She turned and ran blindly. If the man on the gangplank stopped her she would beat him and kick him and scream like Micky and say her mother and father were on board, and her brother and sister and auntie and uncle. She ran.

The busload of schoolchildren were all trailing up the gangway, about fifty of them, laughing and jeering because they were nearly too late. The teachers were at the top hurrying them, the ticketman laughing, the papers in his hand. Milly followed close behind them, all ready to meet the ticketman, all ready to scream, her panics quivering almost beyond her control, worse—far worse—than at any time in the whole journey, because now it was desperate. Now that Micky was on board it was really desperate.

She inched up the gangway, pushing against the children ahead of her, until she was right by the ticketman, the last one.

She opened her mouth. The man put his arm around her kindly and guided her over the step.

"That's all of them. All present and accounted for."

He straightened up and said to the teacher, "Better you than me."

The teacher was a very square, brown-eyed woman with straight fair hair and sensible shoes. She gave Milly a hard look but said not a word. Milly walked along the deck as if in a dream, hardly feeling as if she was touching ground at all, overwhelmed by a feeling of peace and happiness, as if she had just entered the pearly gates of paradise. Not having had to scream and punch and kick her way on board had left her in a trance of

bewilderment. She wanted to cry now, with relief and happiness. It was done! The great, awful journey was accomplished. The gangway was being trundled away, the great doors had closed upon the cargo of cars and trucks and the sailors were casting off the mooring ropes. As she watched, a strip of water appeared between the ship and the pier, growing steadily wider and wider. It was a beautiful sight, the blue water taking over from the harbor flotsam, the white wake drawing out behind with the seagulls hovering over, crying out their French squawks in farewell.

When she found Micky she leaned over the rail with him, watching France recede. Then he wanted to go and look at the cars in the hold, so she made a place where they could meet and impressed it on his mind. It was in the sun on deck at the back, beside a lifeboat. He went away and she lay down on a bench looking at the sky, feeling wonderful. She could not believe that it was only that same morning they had awakened in the antelope pen. It seemed like a century ago. She went to sleep, feeling it must be time. She slept deeply, dreamlessly, the sleep of exhaustion.

When she awoke she could not remember where she was and had an instant's panic again, opening her eyes to the infinity of a violet, afternoon sea, the thud of the engines in her ears, and the shouting and laughing of children. But the panic gave way to relief, remembering. She smiled at her incredible achievement. She sat up slowly, still smiling.

There was a square, brown-eyed woman sitting on a seat opposite hers, watching her. Milly saw who she was, and looked away quickly, slightly worried. There was something about the way the woman was watching, not idle at all, but sharp. She was an interferer, Milly decided heavily, and got up to go.

The woman said, "Are you alone?"

Milly paused, the woman not being the sort one could easily ignore.

"No."

"You've slept there for three hours, and no one has come near you. You came on board alone."

"My brother is here." Milly hoped the woman would think Micky was twenty-one, at least. "I'm traveling with my brother."

At that moment Micky appeared, looking even younger than six—more like four—and said, "I'm hungry. I've been hungry for ages."

Milly glowered at him.

The woman said, "Is that your brother?"

"No," Milly said.

"I am," Micky said crossly.

"Are your parents here?"

"No. They're meeting us at the other end."

"I'm hungry," Micky said.

The woman looked from one to the other of them, with far more interest than Milly liked. Then she got up.

"Would you like a meal? Fish-and-chips? I'm going down there now. You can come with me, if you like."

She did not sound cross at all, but quite friendly. Milly was surprised, and felt strange quite suddenly, as if an enormous, heavy weight had lifted slightly from her back. As if she might not have to do all her own worrying for the time being. Not have to worry about whether their French coins were enough for fish-and-chips or what they were going to do when they got to wherever they were going—and she didn't really know where they

105

were going to exactly. It would be lovely not to have to worry any more. Even to find Fred, and have him do the worrying.

They went down some steps into a big dining room and the woman sat them down at a table against a window and told them to wait. They sat looking at the sea, swinging their legs.

"Who's she?" Micky asked.

"I don't know."

When she came back, with three plates of fish-and-chips and three cups of tea, she said her name was Miss Farmer and she was a teacher traveling with grade 5C of Mayberry Avenue School.

"Of which school you are not a pupil, although you are traveling on our ticket," she said pointedly to Milly, who concentrated hard on her fish-and-chips.

"Aren't you?"

Polite, blank stare. Perhaps now she could pretend she was French, Milly thought. But it was too late.

"You are traveling alone, the two of you?"

Milly nodded.

"You must tell me why, else I shall take you to the captain. You may eat your fish-and-chips first, though."

She was a very amiable lady; even her threat was amiable—firm but friendly. Milly decided it would do no harm if she knew the whole story, for the ship was not going to turn around—of that she was sure. Going home to England was quite definitely what they were doing: the object of the adventure was achieved. The adventure was over. And very glad Milly felt about it and told Miss Farmer the story without regret, when her plate was empty and the last drop of ketchup wiped up by the last chip.

Miss Farmer listened gravely. If she was surprised, she did not show it.

She said, "Your aunt and uncle must be terribly worried about you."

"They didn't want us."

"But they were responsible for you. Perhaps you don't understand what that means. Even if they were not very sympathetic, they would feel dreadful when you disappeared and no one could find you. They will be very frightened for you. I think we should tell the captain and see if he can send a message to the police at St. Malo, to say you are safe."

Seeing the expression on Milly's face, she added, "Don't worry. I will see that you get home safely."

There was something very reassuring about Miss Farmer. She was not a fusspot. She was not cross. She had a penetrating look, but her face was cheerful, not angry and anxious like some teachers'.

"Can I come to the captain?" Micky asked.

"Yes. We'll go and see the purser first, and ask him if we can see the captain."

She took them along to an office where there was a man with a smart uniform and lots of gold braid. After that they were passed on to another man with gold braid, and he escorted them through a door marked "Private" and down a long corridor to a door marked "Captain." It was empty, but they waited in there for a bit, and then the man came back with the captain. They all stood up. The captain was quite young, Milly was surprised to see, younger than the other men with gold braid.

"Stowaways, I hear?" he said, but quite cheerfully. "These are the missing kids then?"

"It seems so," Miss Farmer said. She told him Milly's story. Micky said to Milly, "We didn't stow away. We just walked on."

"Well, don't say anything," Milly said, a great believer in not saying anything. It had been easier in France, with a foreign language, but now there was no excuse for not understanding.

But, expecting wrath and trouble, to Milly's surprise nobody seemed much put out, more amused, almost respectful, and quite surprisingly practical.

"We'll get the message to France, no problem. The guardians will be told by the police that the children are safe."

"And I'll see that the children get back to London. I will contact the local social services if I cannot find their mother."

"Fred's number—" Milly said, and gave it plainly, as she had been taught.

Miss Farmer was most impressed.

"He knows you well?"

"Oh, yes."

"Do you run away often?"

"Sometimes. But only to home. Not *away*."

"Just back," the captain said. "Like homing pigeons." He laughed. "Not running away, but homing."

He put out his hand. "It's a pleasure to meet you." Milly and Micky shook it, flattered. "Have a nice trip."

Milly half thought he might ask them for some money to pay for it, but he didn't. He shook hands with Miss Farmer.

"We'll go and buy some chocolate," Miss Farmer said.

Things were really very satisfactory.

Miss Farmer turned out to be a do-gooder in the Fred mold, not spectacular and snappy, but doggedly hopeful that things might improve slowly. She and Fred seemed to get along very well. They drank a lot of cups of tea in the kitchen, then decided to ring up the hospital to see if Milly and Micky's mother was ready to come home.

"If they're back, I'm coming," she said.

The next day she arrived. She was frightfully

impressed with Milly's journey home and said thoughtfully, "You're a fine one for traveling—just like your father!"

Milly wasn't sure if this was meant as a compliment or not, but her mother hugged her and said, "We'll make sure we all stay together after this. Worried to death I was, wondering about what you were up to."

"Yes, we'll make quite sure you do," Fred said, and offered Miss Farmer another cup of tea.

"Home's best," Milly said.

"Yes, you're right," her mother said. "Pity we can't make your father think that way."

"Come now, you're better off without him," Fred said.

Milly had heard all this before, and the familiarity of it made her feel pleased, that home was never going to change. She liked things to stay the same.

Fred and Miss Farmer came often and stayed talking in the kitchen, playing games with Micky.

The only thing that did change was that Micky stopped screaming. And that was one thing Milly didn't mind one bit. All in all, she thought they had done rather well.